The Universe of Us

Also by Lang Leav

Love & Misadventure
Lullabies
Memories

The Universe of Us

LANG LEAV

Andrews McMeel
Publishing®

a division of Andrews McMeel Universal

Andrews McMeel Publishing
a division of Andrews McMeel Universal
1130 Walnut Street, Kansas City, Missouri 64106

www.andrewsmcmeel.com

16 17 18 19 20 RR2 10 9 8 7 6 5 4 3 2 1

ISBN: 978-1-4494-8012-7

Library of Congress Control Number: 2016941971

Editor: Patty Rice
Designer, Art Director: Diane Marsh
Production Manager: Cliff Koehler
Production Editor: Erika Kuster

The Fell Types are digitally reproduced by Igino Marini.
www.iginomarini.com

ATTENTION: SCHOOLS AND BUSINESSES
Andrews McMeel books are available at quantity discounts
with bulk purchase for educational, business, or sales
promotional use. For information, please e-mail the Andrews
McMeel Publishing Special Sales Department:
specialsales@amuniversal.com.

For Michael, my universe.

INTRODUCTION

*Magic tumbled from her pretty lips and when she spoke the
language of the universe—the stars sighed in unison.*
         —MICHAEL FAUDET

I believe we think more deeply about the universe when we're falling
in love. I think the mysterious pull that draws you to another person
is identical to the one that moves our eyes upward to the stars.

The Universe of Us is my fourth book. As a child, I always loved
the romance of the night sky. While writing this new body of work,
I revisited that sense of wonder and fascination that I have held as
far back as I can remember. The sentiment can be best described as
a mixture of nostalgia and longing.

In many ways, a book is, in itself, a tiny universe. Each page is like
a newly formed galaxy, fashioned from a single, pulsing thought.
A book travels for days, for years, sometimes for centuries to meet
you at an exact point in time.

I hope you enjoy *The Universe of Us* as much as I have enjoyed
putting it together. I like to think it has found you for a reason,
even if that reason is only to draw your eyes skyward once more.

Much love,
Lang

We drift from star to star,
your soul and mine
as one.

We fall nearer to the moon—
we fly closer to the sun.

How We Began

It was how we began. Your mouth against mine, your fingers tracing along the back of my neck.

You asked me to imagine what it must have been like, for the first two people who fell in love; before the word *love* was conceived.

You said it felt like that for you. Like we existed in a time before love——as though we were waiting for the word to catch up to the feeling.

WHAT I WOULD TELL YOU

To you, love was about multitudes.
To me, love was inordinate.

> *I love you*, I would say.
> *How much?* you would ask.

I couldn't find the words to answer you then. But they have found their way to me since. And this is what I would tell you.

I would blanket the world in utter darkness; I would pull back the veil of light and reveal to you a blinding crescendo of stars.

I would drain all the seven seas and ask you to count—one by one—every grain of sand that clings to the ocean floor.

I would tally the beat of every human heart that has echoed since the dawn of our becoming.

And as you look in awe at the sheer magnitude of my admission, I would take your hand in mine and tell you; if only you had let me, this is how much I could have loved you.

DISTANCE

It was all I wanted for the longest time——to open my eyes and see you there. To stretch out my hand and touch the soft, yielding warmth of your skin. But now I have learned the secret of distance. Now I know being close to you was never about the proximity.

I LOVED HIM

I loved how his eyes danced merrily,
    and the gentle way he spoke;
    the way he filled my aimless days,
    with bitterness and hope.

I loved him as I fell to sleep,
    and each morning as I woke;
    I loved him with all my wayward heart—
    until the day it broke.

FIRST SNOW

I fell in love on the third kiss, the first snow, the last slow dance. Ask me what day we met and I can only smile and shake my head. It could have been a Tuesday or the death anniversary of a beloved monarch and I wouldn't have a clue. Our love story comes to me in waves, in movie stills and long summer afternoons spent under a sky of incessant blue. I still think of your eyes in flashes of color, your hands in a frenetic, feverish blur—your smile a mosaic of light and shadow. I still find myself lost in those moments of abstraction.

A Postcard

To the man I love, to my future.

The first time I felt your presence, I began joining the dots in the sky, wondering when our stars would align.

I often think of where you are and if you're happy. Are you in love? I hope she is gentle. I know you and I are the same in that way—we bruise a little more easily than most. You see, our souls were made in the same breath.

I know I'm running late—I'm sorry. Things haven't worked out the way I planned. But believe me when I tell you I am on my way.

Until then, think of me, dream of me and I will do the same. One day I will learn your name, and I will write it somewhere on this page. And we will realize that we have known each other all along.

RECOGNITION

I've never met you before, but I recognize this feeling.

SOMEONE LIKE YOU

Do you think there is the possibility of you and I? In this lifetime, is that too much to hope for? There is something so delicate about this time, so fragile. And if nothing ever comes of it, at least I have known this feeling, this wonderful sense of optimism. It is something I can always keep close to me—to draw from in my darkest hour like a ray of unspent sunshine. No matter what happens next, I will always be glad to know there is someone like you in the world.

TO KNOW HIM

If you want to know his heart, pay close attention to what angers him.

If you want to know his mind, listen for the words that linger in his silence.

If you want to know his soul, look at where his eyes are when you catch him smiling.

YOUR LIFE

You've wandered off too far,
    you've forgotten who you are;
    you've let down the ones you love,
    you've given up too much.

You once made a deal with time,
    but it's slipping by too fast;
    you can't borrow from the future,
    to make up for the past.

You forsake all that you hold dear,
    for a dream that is not your own;
    you would rather live a lie—
    than live your life alone.

I Am

He said loving me was like seeing the ocean for the first time. Watching the waves crash senselessly against the rocks, over and over. Grabbing fistfuls of sand as it trickled through his fingers, like my hair, brittle as ebony, strong and taut like the bumps of his knuckles. He said it was like swallowing his first mouthful of the sea—the sudden shock of betrayal.

He said loving me was like panning for gold. Sifting through arsenic, waist-deep in toil. Lured by the shimmer and promise of transcendence, like the river between my lips, a floodgate that opens for him—only when I choose.

And I told him, if I am so hard to love, then let me run wild. My love is not a testament to my surrender. I will show you just how much I love you, with the inward draw of every breath— the collective sigh of the world and all its despair. But I will never give you what you want in chains.

CHOOSE LOVE

My mother once said to me there are two kinds of men you'll meet. The first will give you the life you want and the second will give you the love you desire. If you're one of the lucky few, you will find both in the one person. But if you ever find yourself having to choose between the two, then always choose love.

TODAY

Today I am not in my skin. My body cannot contain me. I am spilling out and over, like a rogue wave on the shore. Today I can't keep myself from feeling like I don't have a friend in the world. And no matter how hard I try, I can't seem to pick myself up off the floor. My demons are lying in wait, they are grinning in the shadows, their polished fangs glinting, knowing today, it will be an easy kill. But tomorrow, tomorrow could be different, and that is what keeps me going today.

THE BUTTERFLY EFFECT

Close your eyes and think about that boy. Tell me how he makes you feel. Let your mind trace over his tired shoulders. Allow your thoughts to linger on that beautiful smile. Take a deep breath and try to put those dark thoughts aside. For once let go of the reins you've wrapped so tightly around your heart. I know you are scared. Who could blame you? Love is a hurricane wrapped inside a chrysalis. And you are a girl walking into the storm.

IMPOSSIBILITY

Do you know the feeling when you're so happy that you can't imagine ever being sad again? Or when you're so sad that you no longer believe you could ever be happy? When you tell me you love me, I always think of that strange emotion— that feeling of impossibility. You say you love me, and you can't imagine a future without me in it, yet all I can think of is how you must have felt the same way once about someone else.

SHOOTING STARS

I want to light a spark tonight, without striking up a memory of you. Please don't send me shooting stars when my mind is a loaded pistol.

PROCESSION

He used to ask me all the time if I was okay. As though he never knew for sure. He would ask me when he was tired or frustrated or when he felt helpless. He would ask me when he was afraid.

He asked me that same question, long after we stopped being lovers—when we became something less yet somehow more. *Are you okay?* He would whisper on the phone late at night, when his girlfriend was asleep or had gone to her mother's for the weekend. *Are you okay?*

He hasn't asked me in years, but I know he still thinks it. I know the question still reverberates in his mind like a broken record and he will keep looking for answers long after there is nothing left to appease him.

It was always the same question, over and over again. Like the start of a procession. And it took me years to recognize the unsaid words that marched silently behind.

Are you okay; *because I love you.*
Are you okay; *because I need you.*
Are you okay; *because I don't know how to live without you.*

THE LONGEST GOOD-BYE

The longest good-bye is always the hardest. Love for the sake of love is the most painful of all protraction.

MOMENTS

That's the tragedy of growing up—knowing you'll run out of feeling something new for the first time. The sad thing is you only get so many of those moments—a handful if you're lucky—and then you spend the rest of your life turning them over in your head.

I think that's why you meant as much to me as you did, why I held on for so long. I didn't know it back then, but you were the last time I would ever feel anything new.

MOMENT OF TRUTH

One day I looked at you and it occurred to me how beautiful your smile was. I heard music in your laughter—I saw poetry in your words. You asked me why I had that look on my face, as though a shadow had fallen across its sun-drenched landscape, heavy with premonition, dark with revelation. The second I tried to tell myself I wasn't in love was the moment I realized I was.

STILL

We may not be in love anymore, but you're still the only one who knows me.

CONVERSATIONS

"Most people want to save the entire world. It's a lovely thought, and I'm not saying it's not a noble pursuit—but it's impossible to save everyone. You just have to pick your little corner of the world and focus your energy there. That's the only way you will ever make a difference."

"But I don't know if I can make a difference. It feels like I am screaming at the top of my lungs, but no one can hear me. No one cares. How can I change anything if I'm completely powerless?"

"You may be powerless now, but there will be a time when you won't be. Don't you see? And that's the time for you to be loud, to tell the world about the changes you want to see, to set them in motion."

THE LAST TIME

When was the last time you said I love you and meant it. When was the last time you heard those words back.

When was the last time you felt like someone knew you and not the person you've been pretending to be. When was the last time you felt like yourself.

When was the last time you heard someone say his name. When was the last time it killed you to hear it.

When was the last time you felt love well up in you like a newly struck spring. Like an outpouring of the soul.

When was the last time he called you beautiful. When was the first.

A LESSON

There is a girl who smiles all the time,
　　to show the world that she is fine.

A boy who surrounds himself with friends,
　　wishes that his life would end.

For those that say they never knew—
　　the saddest leave the least of clues.

SAHARA

And the weather was so damn sick of being predictable; I heard it began snowing in the Sahara and I wanted to tell you that I've changed.

Aftermath

I want to talk about the aftermath of love,
    not the honeymoon or the hitherto;
    but the upshot and the convalescence,
    the slow, hard hauling—the heavy tow.

I want to tell you about those evenings,
    that crept inside like a vagrant cat;
    and cast around its drawn out shadow,
    untoward—insufferably black.

I want to write about the mornings,
    the sterility of the stark, cold light;
    struck against a pair of bare shoulders,
    the lurid whisper of a misspent night.

I want to convey the afternoon setting,
    the water torture of the sink;
    drip by drip, the clock and its ticking,
    and too much time left now to think.

CROSSROADS

It was a quiet love, a tacit love. It came without prelude or preamble. We never said the word *love*—we didn't have to. It was in our laughter, in the sense of wonder we found in each other. And if we had doubts then, time has told us otherwise.

It was a gentle love, a tactile love. It was all hands and lips and hearts in tandem. There was motion in our bodies and emotion in our discourse. We were a symphony of melody and melancholy. When you find peace in another's presence, there is no mistaking.

It was a kind love, a selfless love. I was a dreamer, and you were a traveler. We met at the crossroads. I saw love in your smile, and I recognized it for the first time in my life. But you had a plane to catch, and I was already home.

POSSIBILITY OF LOVE

Yes, I think it is entirely possible to fall in love with someone you've never met. Physicality is an expression of intimacy—not an indication of it.

DARK MATTER

If you know love like I know love when it is full and ready—
like the pulse knows the tip of the blade before the cut—the
blood rushing to greet its serrated edge. You would know love
like I have if you have seen the sun in every possible gradation
of light; if you can hear the birdsong beyond the rudimentary
call—if you can distinguish between each cadence as it quivers
through the air. If you get so cold sometimes that it burns or
the heat gets so bad your teeth start to chatter—then you will
open up your arms and take this dark thing into the fold and
you will know love like I know love.

FOR THE WORLD

I talk to you all the time, even if you can't hear me. I tell you constantly, over and over, how much I miss you and that for me, nothing has changed. I think about the days when we could say anything to each other. My heart is like a time capsule—it keeps safe the memory of you. I know it's harder with you gone than if you had never been here at all—but I wouldn't have missed it for the world.

A WINTER LOVE

We were like
    the raging sea,
    a winter love
    that could not be.

Our voices were
    the ocean's roar,
    we cried until
    we could cry no more.

We mocked the storms
    and they fell the trees,
    our broken limbs
    among scattered leaves.

The tides had shown
    what we did not heed,
    the water holds—
    and then recedes.

HER TIME

She has been feeling it for awhile——that sense of awakening. There is a gentle rage simmering inside her, and it is getting stronger by the day. She will hold it close to her——she will nurture it and let it grow. She won't let anyone take it away from her. It is her rocket fuel and finally, she is going places. She can feel it down to her very core——this is her time. She will not only climb mountains——she will move them too.

THE CHAOS OF LOVE

I have walked through the ruins of an empire as it fell through the passageway of time. I have witnessed star after star exploding like fireworks, as I fixed my gaze light-years into the sky. And I was only a pinprick of dust on the day they split the atom. I had yet to learn the most destructive thing in the world is the quiet yearning between two people who long to find their way back to each other.

ANYTHING ELSE

I want to plant a seed in your mind, some tiny particle of thought that bears a remnant of me. So little by little, day by day, you find yourself thinking of me, until one morning, you will wake up and realize you can't think of anything else.

KNOW ME

I remember when I met you
    the hands of time stood still;
    you and your camera smile—
    a flash of something real.

We talked until the evening,
    the moon came out for awhile;
    the clock resumed its ticking
    and my heart was on the dial.

The morning came to claim you,
    and as far as I can tell—
    there will never be another,
    who will know me quite as well.

WHEN

When did you stop caring? he asked.
When did you start noticing? she replied.

A FIELD OF FLOWERS

He spoke to her once about a field of flowers and a warm spring day. He, with his thoughts spilled onto paper, and she, with a sketchbook and pencil in hand. And she pictured them there, with her head on his shoulder and his hand resting on her thigh. She heard the contented chatter of birds and the slow, rhythmic hum of bees. If she could describe happiness to you, it would be that vision he conjured up for her. If she could take from all the possibilities, that moment would be the one she would bring into fruition. And yet the world spins too quickly and it turns too slowly as she waits and waits for the dream to transact into memory. Until the day comes when she can no longer tell the difference.

UNTIL IT'S GONE

"Some people don't know what they have until it's gone."

"But what about the ones who do know? The ones who never took a damn thing for granted? Who tried their hardest to hold on, yet could only look on helplessly while they lost the thing they loved the most.

"Isn't it so much worse for them?"

THE ONE

I don't want you to love me because I'm good for you, because I say and do all the right things. Because I am everything you have been looking for.

I want to be the one that you didn't see coming. The one who gets under your skin. Who makes you unsteady. Who makes you question everything you have ever believed about love. Who makes you feel reckless and out of control. The one you are infuriatingly and inexplicably drawn to.

I don't want to be the one who tucks you into bed—I want to be the reason why you can't sleep at night.

JUPITER'S MOON

I had a dream last night where you and I were standing on the surface of Jupiter's moon. We ascended weightless and free, our bodies no longer tethered to the rules of gravity.

Take my hand and come with me. Let's go to Callisto. Our feet will never have to touch the ground.

LOVER'S PARADOX

Tell me that story again—the one where the world ends how
it began with a boy who loves a girl and a girl who loves a boy.
And she is deaf and he is blind and he tells her he loves her
over and over and she writes him every day but never hears a
thing back.

ALL I WANT

I'm not asking for a grand declaration of love. I've stopped entertaining those thoughts long ago. You see, I have resigned myself to where I am now, hanging by a thin, tenuous thread. I can feel it twisting above me, gently fraying, slowly giving way. I'm not asking for promises or tenure—I just want a hand to reach for at the breaking point.

THE REDWOOD TREE

My father once told me a story about an old redwood tree—how she stood tall and proud—her sprawling limbs clothed in emerald green. With a smile, he described her as a mere sapling, sheltered by her elders and basking in the safety of the warm, dappled light. But as this tree grew taller, she found herself at the mercy of the cruel wind and the vicious rain. Together, they tore relentlessly at her pretty boughs, until she felt as though her heart would split in two.

After a long, thoughtful pause, my father turned to me and said, "My daughter, one day the same thing will happen to you. And when that time comes, remember the redwood tree. Do not worry about the cruel wind or the vicious rain—but do as that tree did and just keep growing."

A WHOLE UNIVERSE

The days catapult before me. The world is spinning too quickly. It gets harder and harder to retrace my steps. To figure out how I got to be here.

The years expand into eons. It gets easier for me to imagine my mother as a girl. To think about her worn-out heart— breaking for the things she couldn't hold on to. And I wonder if I've let the wrong people go. When you lose a person, a whole universe goes along with them.

Sometimes I picture all my other selves, standing in line like a row of dominoes; separate but part of the same disjointed whole. How can I hold a single one accountable? No one ever walks away from love, knowing they can never go back.

HEROES

I was never one to believe in superheroes. I always thought they belonged solely within the pages of a book. Until the day one showed up in my life and changed my point of view.

Like some fairy-tale knight, he turned up when I needed him the most. He pulled me out of the mire with his big, strong arms and for the first time in awhile, I felt solid ground beneath my feet. I was as unsteady as a newborn—it was as though my legs had forgotten the simple task of walking. And I clung to him like he was the second coming, and I was the world's newest convert.

I think he hung up his cape a long time ago. I can signal my torch against the window or send a flare up into the sky, and it wouldn't make a difference. No one is coming to save me this time. I guess I'll just have to save myself.

EPIPHANY

Here are the words that have brought me to a new understanding. Here are the words that will bind us forever. From this day forward, I will speak your name with gratitude, knowing it is the mantra of my soul. I will let you go, knowing we are eternal. We were born to walk this world in intersecting lines. We are circles and signposts and parallels. I have left markers for you at every turn. Look for me in everything that catches your breath. Let the simple miracle of your own presence overwhelm you. For you are beautiful, in ways that can't be described. And we are love at its most inexplicable. With these words, I am one with divinity. With these words, I am one with you.

ODE TO WRITERS

The greatest plight
　　of one who writes
　　is the irrational fear,
　　that what they write
　　possibly won't—
　　ever be quite as good
　　as what they wrote.

GONE

"The sad thing is," she said, "the moment you start to miss someone, it means they're already gone."

AN INSOMNIAC'S DREAM

I missed you today. Between waking and sleeping, I thought of you.

We met somewhere inside an insomniac's dream, in a world so precarious—it could crumble at any given time—folding at the slightest touch.

I wish I could have a day with you, where the sun never went past noon. Or a night, where the stars could go on forming their constellations; until the sky was filled with stories of how I loved you.

You once told me that you had to bend time and space to be at my side. But it would only be for a moment, you had said.

How long? I asked.

But it was already over, long before the answer could leave your lips.

ONCE

I loved you once and now I must spend my whole life
explaining why.

TOO MUCH

Are you like me? Do you give too much, too quickly? Do you throw yourself blindly at the world, thinking that it will always open its arms up to you?

Do you feel the slow turning beneath your feet, the shifting plates? Do you sense the streams of fissures roaring underneath like unrequited love, desperate for somewhere to go?

Do you feel the wind pulling back and forth, constricting and expanding, a perpetual cycle as vicious as it is tender, like when it hurts you to breathe but it's the only thing that sustains you?

Are you like me? Do you live with the dial turned up at full volume? Can you taste the salt of the sea when you're miles inland and the ocean feels like a fractured memory?

Are you like me? Are you alive or just pretending?

DARK THOUGHTS

My idle hands
    and restless mind—
    into darkness,
    begin to delve.

Seldom do I think of you,
    but today I thought
    of little else.

AWAKE

I was loved in my dreams last night. It echoed through me like thunder—I felt it through and through.

When I woke up, I couldn't shake the feeling of his arms around me and the sound of his voice, already half forgotten.

The loss was indescribable. And I couldn't help that feeling of certainty that I have felt this way before. Somewhere in time, throughout the ages, I was loved—I was loved and my eyes were wide open.

HER LOVE LETTERS

The truth is there are pieces of me in everything I have written
to you, for you. After all, what is a poet but a composite of her
love letters?

I WILL CRY

Tomorrow I'll cry for all the world,
    for all the things gone wrong;
    I will cry for every tethered bird,
    who has lost her joyful song.

Tomorrow I'll cry for every heart,
    that has broken, like boughs, in two,
    but today, my love, you have my tears—
    today I will cry for you.

SALVE

"You've made your choice, and there's nothing I can do," she said. "I don't think you want me in your life anymore, and I have to find a way to live with that. You said you would still be there for me, but I don't want to be a mere courtesy—a salve for your guilt. You won't hear from me again after today, and I don't want you to worry. I'll be okay. Because I have to be."

TIME STANDS STILL

In cemeteries
    of memories
    our love will lie
    in caskets.

My time with he
    an eternity—
    neither present
    nor future
    can past it.

My heart still kept
    where it was left—
    if ever he were
    to ask it.

TERRITORY

I think there is a sense of ownership in knowing, isn't there? You let people in, and they claim parts of you—they fly their flag over uncharted territory and from then onward—you cease to belong wholly to yourself.

A PREMONITION

There are some people who you look at, and you can just tell how their story will end. I don't know what it is; they have everything going for them, yet it will never be enough. But when I look at you, I just know instinctively, that despite the odds against you and although life will always find a way to test you, someday you'll have everything you want. Your ending will be a happy one.

NINE LIVES

Does the past ever appear before you, like a bolt in the blue? Something or someone from many lives ago. It knocks you right off your feet, just when you thought you'd found solid ground. But it's only an illusion, isn't it? All this time, the plates have been shifting beneath you and the world keeps spinning round and round like the plates in a circus act. Yet you still can't leave it behind; that one thing that was kept from you. No matter what you are given, it still scratches at the corner of your mind, like a cat begging to be let in.

BLUE

You begin to invent things after awhile. I suppose it's only human nature to add and subtract from our memories; to recall them the way we feel they should be remembered. After all, our lives are a living work of art—shouldn't we be allowed to shape it in any way we choose?

I remember the first time I saw my favorite painting, how its fragile beauty caught my breath. And I thought if the artist had painted just one brushstroke less, he could have told an entirely different story. If he began with a smear of red instead of blue, it could have been a chapter instead of an era.

SELF-LOVE

Once when I was running,
    from all that haunted me;
    to the dark I was succumbing—
    to what hurt unbearably.

Searching for the one thing,
    that would set my sad soul free.

In time I stumbled upon it,
    an inner calm and peace;
    and now I am beginning,
    to see and to believe,
    in who I am becoming—
    and all I've yet to be.

THE EDGE OF THE WORLD

You think falling in love is about holding on, but it isn't. It is about hands gripping the edge of the world and letting go, one finger at a time.

Take a deep breath—here comes the drop. I know it's your first time here, but soon you will get used to the motion; the headlong dive into the deep. Just go with it. You only get one chance to fall in love with your heart still whole.

THE LONELIEST PLACE

I believe there is penance in yearning. There is poverty in giving away too much of your heart. When the desire for another is not returned in equal measure—nothing in the world could compensate for the shortfall. Sometimes the loneliest place to be is in love.

A BEAUTIFUL COLLISION

There was a feeling of inevitability when I met you. The sense that we would be together; that there would be a moment when you would look at me in a certain way, and we would cross the threshold from friendship into something so much more.

We spoke once about lovers who kept finding each other, no matter how many times the world came between them. And I think I had to break your heart, and you had to break mine. How else could we know the worth of what we were given?

I think you were always meant to know me a little better than anyone else. And our lives were fated to converge like some cosmic dance. I know there is a terrible distance between us. But our bodies are made of stardust, and we are hurtling through space and time, toward the most beautiful collision.

HEART AND MIND

Do you think the mind answers to the heart? The way it keeps conjuring up what is no longer there. When in love, we swing like a pendulum between the two. We want the mirage knowing it will never be enough. But the heart does not have eyes and the mind cannot resist when it asks, *tell me just one more time.*

Wandering Star

She walks the earth freely, yet her feet never touch the ground. Many hands will reach for her, but she cannot be anchored. She belongs to no one, to nothing, to nowhere. When you meet her, you will recognize her for who she is —a free spirit, a wandering star. She will fit in your arms like she was made to be there. And she will show you what it means to hold something you can never hold on to.

WITHIN MY REACH

I wish the love
    I have come to meet,
    was not an inch
    within my reach.

I wish the prize
    was so far-flung,
    that I would not cry
    if it were not won.

I wish the dream
    was placed so high
    that my panicked heart—
    would dare not try.

QUIET

I've grown quiet now. You won't hear me talk about you anymore. It doesn't hurt like it used to. I suppose that is something to be thankful for.

I will never be the girl I was before I knew you. On some days, I miss her, more than I miss you. After all, she was the one you fell desperately in love with, even if you didn't know it at the time.

You've grown quiet too. I don't think it's for a lack of things to say. Sometimes, things don't work out the way we plan. What's the point in dwelling on what could have been?

I went to sleep last night, thinking about you. Life is just a dream after all. Come and find me when you wake up.

ALL I ASK

Life: a question,
    death: its reply—
    a tender good-bye.

Stay 'til our present
    slips into the past—
    it is all that I ask.

Torn

Some days I feel like my soul is being pulled in one direction and my heart in another.

LOVING YOU

Loving you is like being ten years old again, scaling a tree with my eyes bright and skyward, wanting only to get higher and higher, without a thought of how I would get back down.

WHAT I HOPE FOR

I am hoping for a sign in the sky or a word from the stars. I am praying for a tear in the fabric of time so you and I can slip quietly away and not a single soul would think to miss us.

THE WEATHER

It was raining on the day I met him—hair wet and tangled—
droplets of water sliding down my cheeks like crystal teardrops.
He says he can taste sunlight on my skin whenever cherries
are in season. With me, he doesn't think about permanence
or possession. He knows I'm just like the weather—I'll keep
changing my mind.

CRYING

You're still crying about him aren't you? Silly girl. What good will it do you to spill those sky blue tears? You meant either everything to him or absolutely nothing at all.

DARK ROOM

Tell someone about me. I can't bear to think that I have vanished from your world completely. I can't stand the thought of resting like a silent tomb in your heart, shut away from the light. I don't want to be an inscription on the first page of your book or the opening of a trilogy. Have you forgotten everything we spoke about? Could you live the rest of your life without speaking my name?

Tell someone about me; even if it hurts. You once told me that everyone has a dark room. Is that where you have put me? Do my photographs still hang on tenuous cords that twist into your memory?

Tell someone about me. Don't let me fade away like a Polaroid. Time can be cruel in that way. But you and I are still living and breathing in this imperfect world. What could be a greater miracle than that?

Tell someone about me. I don't want our story to end here, and your words may be the only thing that can save us. Relinquish your pride for just one moment—put an end to this interminable silence and tell someone about me. Or tell the whole world.

ORIGAMI

He says that I am ivory and indifference. My eyes are cold and hard like sapphires but behind their wintry gaze, there is a murmur of a girl. He takes my trembling hands in his and tells me I am safe with him. His touch is sweet like a memory of something long gone and I want to fold myself into his arms like origami. He says that I am paper, lily-white, and he will spoil me with words if I let him.

SOLACE

When all I desired
    was once promised
    to me.

And all have conspired
    to keep it
    from reach.

There is safety in numbness—
    there is solace
    in sleep.

·

CONTACT

It was the longest she had gone without human contact; without the soft, conceding warmth of someone else's skin. She began to crave it after awhile, to obsess over the most trivial things. Like a hand on her shoulder or a kind word from a stranger. How long, she wonders, before I forget how it feels to be wanted? How long until I lose all recollection of love?

My Heartache

If this is my heartache, then let it be mine to endure. Permit me to feel it in its entirety. Don't tell me how much of you I am allowed to love.

HANSEL

A feast upon
    I feasted on
    when my eyes
    first looked at you.
    While deep inside
    as I looked on,
    a hunger grew
    and grew.

The time we spent
    came and went,
    as you slipped
    from me
    like hours.

Now I seek of you,
    a speck of you,
    left for me
    to devour.

The crumbs you threw,
    the trails to you,
    I believed they led—
    were in my head.

The crumbs you threw,
    will make me ill—
    yet they are all,
    I have of you.

The banquet done,
    for all but one,
    as the crumbs
    grow fewer and few.

My love will flow
    on and on,
    while slowly
    I am starved of you.

One Day

One day she began talking to him again. After seven long
years of silence, there it was, her voice on the other end of
the phone, soft and lilting. She had one of those voices that
reminded him of a wormhole. The power it possessed to close
all that time and distance between them, the way it brought
her back to him once more—tenuous and shimmering—like
a dewdrop catching the sun.

THE ESSENCE

I saw a swaying tree,
    I felt it sway in me.

A bird trilled out her song,
    To me this song belongs.

What's given is not gone—
    in something it lives on.

THE GIRL SHE WAS

She doesn't feel like herself. Not anymore. She was different once.

Now she is like a watered-down version, pale and thin. She slips through the cracks unnoticed. She fades into the background, afraid of saying the wrong thing. She grows sharp edges and won't let anyone get close to her.

She doesn't know how she came to be like this, how she ended up here. She only remembers the way she used to be—wild and reckless. Bold and unapologetic.

YOUR WORDS

Remember, your words are your power. Never forget your words.

4000 MILES

The lines stitched into highways,
    the never-ending seams;
    on roads that are less traveled,
    dividing you and me.

I wish I could unravel
    the fabric in-between,
    and tear away the distance,
    to bring you close to me.

TALK AGAIN

I want us to talk again—the way we used to when the sun was coming up, and we were miles away from anywhere.

I want us to talk again—about all the things we would think about, yet never thought to say out loud to anyone else.

I want us to talk again—like the way we did before we wanted to do anything more than that. I want us to talk.

And if we never talk again, I want you to know that I miss that most of all—and every time the sun goes down, I think of all the things I wish I could tell you.

BREAKING UP

You think it happens when you've stopped caring. When all the tenderness and warmth are stripped away and all that's left is cold and empty and broken.

But you never imagine it will happen like this. With our arms around each other, our hearts full of love and neither of us wanting to be the first to let go.

ONE THING

She looked up at the sky and whispered, take anything away from me, take it all if you want to; but please—please just let me keep this one thing.

CHASING BUTTERFLIES

She flitted in and out of his life like a recurring dream. Even when she was an arm's length away—it felt like she was somewhere else. He would reach out and touch her and his hand would come away empty.

AND THEN

I always thought the words *and then* were a prelude to something wonderful. Like seeing a ship come in or finding a note in your letterbox, when you weren't expecting one. That swift, surprising transition from nothing to everything.

And then.

Two little words that hold a world of promise.

And then the light pierced through the dark, forbidding sky, and the rain stopped falling.

And then I met you.

JUMP

"Don't you get it?" he said. "The ones who are afraid of heights don't trust themselves enough not to jump."

LONELINESS

I don't know when I last caught myself staring at the clock. It must have been before the hour hand began turning for somebody else. Since then I have become a deft collector of minutes, like a caged bird hungry for the sky. Do you know I have thoughts that could color all the oceans blue? Those who harbor dreams of being alone must have forgotten what loneliness is.

PUNISHED

"We were happy," she said, and her eyes, downcast and brimming, reminded him of how the sky was before the first splash of rain. "We were happy and they punished us for it."

CIRCLES

My mind, a Venn diagram.
    You, the overlap and the intersect;
    a pulsating glimmer——omnipresent,
    a lighthouse with its glowing breath.

You are the stone that skirts the river,
    that skips along its crystal plane;
    a surface skimmed by concentric shimmer,
    and trembles with the touch of rain.

You are worlds that spin in orbit,
    a star who rose and fell;
    infinity summoned for audit——
    a penny toss in the wishing well.

CONTRITION

There was a look in his eyes I had never seen before. And it took me a few moments to recognize it for what it was. *Remorse.*

I don't deserve you, he said, half-defeated, half-hopeful. It was the most honest thing he had ever said to me. And he was right. He didn't deserve me. Not by a long shot. But he had me nonetheless.

YOUR DARKEST SELF

I think love is about being your darkest, most destructive self.
To be loved, not in spite of this but because of it.

COLLISION COURSE

Tomorrow I will tell you that I love you. Nothing in the world can stop the maddening rush of those three words. *I love you.* I know you were born with your heart already broken. But the world began in pieces and somehow made itself whole.

Tell me where to put the stars. Show me how the oceans keep spilling over. Your smile is a blazing trail of light, shot down from the heavens. And I know how much this is going to hurt. But it's too late for me to get off this collision course. Tomorrow I will tell you that I love you. And nothing in the world can stop the maddening rush of those three words.

HE

He is the thought behind the feeling,
    the swelling in my chest;
    the starlight in the evening,
    the yearning when I undress.

He is the sound behind the sighing,
    the song of every bird;
    the tears in all my crying,
    the ache in every word.

PREDESTINED STARS

He and I collided like two predestined stars and in that brief moment I felt what it was like to be immortal.

KEY TURN

There we were at the breaking point when you told me you could explain everything if I would just let you. But I wouldn't. That was the moment I chose to pull the door between us firmly shut.

I always wonder what you would have said if I had let you continue. Perhaps there was something in your explanation that would have allowed me to trust you again—that would have made sense of it all. As unlikely as that scenario could have been, my mind remains firmly hinged on the possibility—the key turn of a chance that maybe, I had it wrong all this time.

THE PERFECT CRIME

It wasn't with knives
    my heart he tore;
    when he brought me
    to death's door.

It wasn't his hands
    that had me slain—
    but he had killed me
    all the same.

Cold and callous
    with no remorse,
    he turned me to
    a walking corpse.

And I am imprisoned
    in this pain,
    while he without
    the slightest blame—
    free to do it
    over again.

WAR ON LOVE

Write about the first thing that comes to your mind; that your heart has longed to remind you. Write about the thrumming rhythm that implicates you—the lingering thoughts that tempt you. Write about the one thing that absolves you.

Write about the peace you've found in denial——the salvage in walking away. It's okay; no one blames you. You can't wage war on love if you don't know your limits.

EROS

If time were governed by Eros, I would stay in your arms forever. If time answered only to lovers, I would never leave your side. The seconds pass by slower when I'm staring at the clock. And you wonder why I can't take my eyes off you.

A Bookstore

Standing in a bookstore, near a street where you used to live, I found myself wishing you would walk through the door and we would meet for the first time—all over again.

THE PIANO

Love was never meant to be black and white. But I knew the truth could free me as my hands were poised over the keys and I could have made them sing, I could have made them sing, but the feeling went away and I lost the courage to tell you.

STITCHES AND SCARS

We all want to be on par,
  to steal the wish
  from someone's star.

Our flaws and failings
  stitches and scars,
  to be loved
  for who we are.

Remorse

You loved her and now you know what you've lost. Now your hands feel emptier than before you met her—your heart feels heavier. But you were young and you were careless. How were you to know the value of what you were given?

Yet a part of you did know. In some strange, mysterious way, you knew there was something special about that girl. In her eyes, you caught a glimpse of your own destiny. You knew it was meant to travel with hers.

If only you could go back to that day; to the one where she stood before you, gentle and hopeful—waiting for you to make up your mind. When you had thought to yourself that nothing could ever look as beautiful.

That was the moment you should have told her what your heart was telling you. If you had allowed it, she could have been your whole world. All you had to do was open the door. All you had to say was, *come in*.

RAVINE

I think maybe we were cursed or just plain unlucky. You had your ideas about love, and I had mine. And as much as we tried, we couldn't make it work. I don't think it was the lack of feeling or intention that broke us—it was one small misunderstanding after another. Isn't it strange how a minor disparity can grow into a ravine? In the end, it was enough to tear us apart.

YOUNG LOVE

Screeching tires, a near miss. A horn blaring sharply into the night. I close my eyes. Here come the flashbacks.

We were losing track of the days and nights, counting fireflies and waiting for the sun to come around. I was so addicted to you. I remember the exquisite fatigue as I fought off sleep for another hit—another line of conversation. We drove down freeways and winding roads, in a sleepless stupor, the stereo blasting love songs that were a cheap imitation of what we were feeling. Sometimes I wished you would take us over the edge, and we would be forever young and crazy in love. Go slow around those curves. I only want you safe now. It doesn't matter if we're together or apart. I love you so much. I'll love you, right until the end.

Acknowledgments

I would like to thank Al Zuckerman and Samantha Wekstein from Writers House for their continued guidance and support.

To Kirsty and her team at Andrews McMeel for their hard work and dedication.

To Oliver Faudet, one of the brightest stars in my universe.

To my family and friends, I am so lucky to have you in my life.

And a very special thank-you to my readers. Your support means the world to me.

ABOUT THE AUTHOR

Lang Leav is the international best-selling author of *Love & Misadventure*, *Lullabies*, and *Memories*. She is the winner of a Qantas Spirit of Youth Award and coveted Churchill Fellowship. Her book *Lullabies* was the 2014 winner of the Goodreads Choice award for poetry.

Lang has been featured in various publications including *The Straits Times*, *The Guardian*, and *The New York Times*. She currently resides in New Zealand with her partner and fellow author, Michael Faudet, in a little house by the sea.

INDEX

Join Lang Leav on the following:

Facebook   Tumblr   Twitter   Instagram